How Gobbly Gobbler and Friends Worked Together to Make a Delicious Dinner

This is a work of fiction. Names, characters, places and incidents either are products of the author's imagination or are used fictitiously. Any resemblance to actual events or locales or persons, living or dead, is entirely coincidental.

Printed in the United States of America

ISBN 979-8-89114-246-6 (sc)
ISBN 979-8-89114-247-3 (e)

Library of Congress Control Number: 2025923223

2026.01.08

MainSpring Books
5901 W. Century Blvd
Suite 750
Los Angeles, CA, US, 90045

www.mainspringbooks.com

How Gobbly Gobbler and Friends Worked Together to Make a Delicious Dinner

Kathleen Whitham

Once upon a time not so long ago, on a Thursday in late November, there was a little gathering in the kitchen of Grandmother's house, conveniently located over the river and through the woods.

The eleven participants were slated to cooperate and work together as a team to come up with an outstanding Thanksgiving meal, but because of a few not-so-positive behavioral tendencies, they got off to a slow start. Members of the group included the following:

- Gobbly Gobbler, the largest member of the group, who appeared to take great pleasure in throwing his ample weight around and had a certain inclination toward bossiness.
- Saucy Cranberry, who was a little too self-satisfied with her beautiful red color and sweet-tart status.
- Sweet Potato, otherwise known as Sweet P, who was happy to remind everyone of her exceptional culinary skills.
- Mashed Potato, who was convinced that he was the most appreciated dish on the menu and said so often.

- Cornbread Stuffing, who was fearful and afraid of many things, especially the dark.
- Gravy, who never tired of repeating, "I've got you covered, I've got you covered."
- Green Bean, who had always been insecure and feared being the last "picked."
- Yeast Roll, who was pleased to express his delight at having his own special plate at the table.

- Pumpkin Pie and her sister, Pecan Pie, also known as P-kin and P-can, who unfortunately had always had some jealousy issues and too often engaged in irritating squabbles over unimportant matters.
- And last but not least, Sweet Tea, who also happened to be positive and sweet-natured and was well aware that great things can be accomplished through group effort and collaboration.

The conversation went as follows:

"Excuse me, everyone," gobbled Gobbly Gobbler loudly and boldly. "Since I'm the biggest one here, I figure I should step up and take charge of this meeting!"

Mashed Potato quickly spoke up, "Just a minute, Gobbly. I believe that size is much less important than popularity, and I've been at the top of the popularity chart for years. I go with everything, so I'm always invited to dinner parties and restaurants."

Cranberry piped in saucily, "Actually, you're kind of plain and boring. Without Gravy, you're not so exciting. But speaking of exciting, I'm a beautiful red color and therefore very—"

Gravy interrupted, "Yeah, Mashy, I've got you covered."

"Thanks, Gravy," responded Mashed Potato. "You and I make a great pair. But, Cranberry, you're not nearly as exciting as you think, and you're only around at Christmas and Thanksgiving anyway."

Green Bean murmured shyly, "Hey, Cranberry, I may be a bit plain and boring myself, but I am green. And I think you and I would make a great red-and-green team to announce the fast-approaching holiday season."

"Thanks, Greenie," replied Cranberry. "I'm totally '*reddie*' for that partnership," she added, smiling at her little play on words.

Cornbread Stuffing, who had always been timid and fearful, chimed in. "Guys, I must admit that I'm feeling very nervous because I'm afraid of the dark, and pretty soon, I'm supposed to be going into the Gobbly Gobbler chamber of darkness for like six hours. I don't like that idea one bit!"

"That's just the way it works," Gobbly responded. "Ha! I'll be 'stuffed' long before dinner even begins," he added, mentally patting himself on the back for his superior sense of humor.

Sweet P joined the conversation boastfully. "It is well known that I'm the queen of cuisine. After all, I am responsible for the best pies, fries, cakes, and casseroles."

"Well, I'm the beast of the yeast," replied Yeast Roll. "And I even get my own private plate. The rest of you have to crowd onto one plate."

"We don't," countered P-kin and P-can, the Pie Sisters, simultaneously. "We're the dessert divas and we get special treatment and private plates as well."

It was Sweet T's turn to speak, and she was getting so steamed up by this conversation that her ice had begun to melt. "Goodness gracious, this is absolutely ridiculous. Don't you realize what Thanksgiving is all about? It's about family and friends and appreciation and being grateful for what you have, the big obvious blessings as well as the smaller not-so-obvious, underappreciated, or unseen ones. Plus, each one of us is an essential part of the whole team. So please, let's put aside our bossiness, our vanity, our petty jealousies, our selfishness, and our insecurities and work together to create an excellent outcome. And in the meantime, let's be thankful for the privilege of being able to do that, and for this holiday, which encourages us to think about being grateful for all the blessings, large and small, that we enjoy throughout the year."

"Here's an idea," proposed Green Bean, who was beginning to feel a bit more confident. "Why don't we all take turns saying something we're thankful for? I understand that this is a common Thanksgiving tradition."

Everyone in the group agreed, and each had a contribution to make.

Sweet T spoke first. "I'll start. If someone's thirsty, I can help out. I'm grateful that I can help others."

Sweet P said, "Well, I'm thankful for my roots (I am a root vegetable after all) and especially for children. I'm so happy to be one of the baby's first solid foods!"

P-kin confessed, "I'm thankful for my pie family, and yes, I must say that I really love and am thankful for my 'nutty' sister."

P-can responded, "Thank you, Sis. I totally love and appreciate you, too, and I'm also thankful for all my pie, cake, and cookie friends, and bakers!"

Gobbly Gobbler declared, "I'm thankful for my animal friends everywhere, be they feathered like me or furry, scaly, smooth, small, medium, large, whatever. Animals provide beauty, natural balance, companionship, service, food, and much more all over the world."

Cranberry added, "I'm thankful for all my fruity friends. We're a very varied bunch, all different kinds of shapes, colors, tastes, origins, and sizes. I love that!"

Cornbread Stuffing continued, "I'm grateful for grains since I'm made from one of the world's main grains along with rice, wheat, and others. We have the honor of helping to feed millions of humans and animals worldwide."

Yeast Roll admitted, "I do enjoy my rockin' role as a roll, which allows me to be a part of many meals. So I'm grateful for friendships and for being included, and I really don't care at all about private plates. It's actually kind of lonely all by myself."

Mashed Potato explained, "I'm thankful for farmers, potato farmers, and *all* farmers. You've heard the expression, 'If you ate today, thank a farmer.' And of course, I greatly appreciate Gravy, my buddy."

Gravy answered, "I appreciate you, too, Mashy, and I am thankful to be working together with all of you, and don't forget, I've got you covered!"

Green Bean summed it up. "First of all, I'm grateful for gardens. Gardens give us healthy food and beautiful flowers and attract other exquisite living things such as bees, butterflies, and birds. And of course, I'm thankful for Thanksgiving and that it's giving us all the opportunity to cooperate and work together to create something beautiful and meaningful."

So right there in Grandmother's kitchen, all eleven of them vowed to make serious strides upward on both the thankfulness meter and the teamwork meter and to work together to make the best and most delicious Thanksgiving meal possible. And guess what, they did!

What are *you* thankful for? Have a wonderful Thanksgiving!

About the Author

Kathleen, a graduate of Indiana University with a master's degree from the University of North Carolina, is a French teacher with over forty years of experience. She is also the owner and chief chef of a pie-making business in Hillsborough, North Carolina. However, she considers her role as mother of five sons and grandmother of eight to be the role of utmost importance in her life. She has written several stories for her grandchildren over the past few years. She chose Thanksgiving as the theme for this story because this holiday celebrates thankfulness and giving and because of her many wonderful memories of Thanksgivings over the years, both at her grandmother's farm in Indiana and with her children and grandchildren in North Carolina.

www.ingramcontent.com/pod-product-compliance
Lightning Source LLC
Chambersburg PA
CBRC102054010826
48978CB00021B/182